I AM READING

MOOSE and MOUSE

WRITTEN AND ILLUSTRATED BY
COLIN WEST

KINGFISHER
BOSTON

To Cathie

KINGFISHER
a Houghton Mifflin Company imprint
222 Berkeley Street
Boston, Massachusetts 02116
www.houghtonmifflinbooks.com

First published in 2004
4 6 8 10 9 7 5 3
3TR/0504/AJT/FR(FR)/115MA/F

LIBRARY OF CONGRESS CATALOGING-IN-PUBLICATION DATA
has been applied for.

ISBN 0-7534-5715-6

Printed in India

Contents

Mouse's Poem

Moose and Mouse were friends.

Moose was big
and strong.

But Mouse was the
one with the brains.

Moose liked outdoor life.

Mouse preferred
life indoors. He
made up poems on
his old typewriter.

One sunny day Moose decided to visit his friend Mouse.

There was a spring in his step as he walked up Mouse's pathway.

"Coming fishing?" asked Moose.

"Too busy!" said Mouse.

"I'm working on a poem."

Moose left Mouse to do his typing.

Moose wandered down to the riverbank.

He found his favorite rock and sat down.

He fished in the river all morning.

Moose caught three big ones!

"*Just the thing for lunch,*" thought
Moose as he fried the three fish.
And they were delicious!

Moose wondered what his friend was
doing for lunch.
"*Maybe he's too busy to make
anything,*" he thought.

"I know Mouse likes fish,"
Moose thought.
So he packed
a bag of leftovers
for his friend.

Then he picked some nice nuts and
berries to go with them.

Moose took the bundle to Mouse's house.

He tapped on the window.

"Hello, Mouse!" he cried.

"I've got a surprise for you."

Mouse frowned.

He didn't look up from his typewriter.

Moose tapped on the window again.

"Yoo hoo!" he shouted.

"I've brought you some lunch!"

"I'm too busy to stop!" snapped Mouse.

"I'm working on my poem."

"I'll leave your lunch on the doorstep,"
said Moose.

"Okay!" said Mouse somewhat angrily.
As Moose was about to leave, he noticed
that Mouse's yard was a complete mess.
There were rotten apples all over the lawn.

"*Maybe Mouse is too busy to clean up,*"
thought Moose.

Moose decided to help out.

He worked hard, picking up the rotten

fruit and putting it in an old sack.

It took him over an hour to finish.

Moose looked in
Mouse's window.
Mouse was still
at his typewriter.
Moose tapped
gently on the glass.

"Hello, Mouse," he said softly.
"I've cleaned up your yard for you."

"Fine!" snapped Mouse.
"I'll see you
tomorrow!"
he added
somewhat rudely.

"Good-bye, then," said Moose.

Moose left the sack by Mouse's door.

He gathered his things and wandered

home to bed.

The next day Moose went to Mouse's house.

He noticed something odd.

The lunch bag was still on the doorstep.

But the sack of rotten apples was

missing!

Moose knocked on Mouse's door.

After awhile it opened.

"Come in," said Mouse weakly.

Mouse looked sick.

"You've been working too hard," said
Moose. Mouse nodded.

"But at least I've finished the poem,"
he muttered.

He showed it to Moose:

Moose is brave,
Moose is strong,
Moose works hard
All day long.

Moose is broad,
Moose is tall,
Moose is my
Best friend of all.

Moose is helpful
As can be,
And he's almost as
Smart as me!

"Wow! You're so smart," said Moose,

beaming with pride.

"Maybe so, but I've got a horrible bellyache," said Mouse sadly. "I think it was that lunch you left me yesterday!"

The End

The Camping Trip

Moose was excited.
At last Mouse had agreed
to go camping with him.

Mouse told Moose about all the things
to pack.
Mouse was good
at remembering
things.

"Thanks for being so helpful,"
said Moose.
He put everything in his backpack, and
they were off.

Mouse wasn't too excited about camping.
He preferred the comfort of his own home.
"I hope the weather holds out," he said as
they left home.

They walked down the path toward
the woods.

"I hope there
aren't any
bears here!"
said Mouse.

"And I hope there
aren't any wolves
either!" he added.

Moose admired the view by the lake.

"How wonderful!" he sighed.

"Humph!" muttered Mouse.

"I've got a better view on my own

wall—a picture of the Bahamas."

They walked into the woods.

"What a lovely sound!" said Moose as he heard a woodpecker.

"Humph!" said Mouse.

"I prefer listening to a good tune on my CD player!"

They reached a clearing at the top

of a hill and stopped for awhile.

Moose breathed in deeply.

"What nice fresh air!" he said.

"If you ask me, it's pretty chilly,"

said Mouse.

"I prefer sitting indoors."

They walked and talked some more.
They watched the sun go down over
the hills.

"It's beautiful," said Moose.

"It's getting dark," observed Mouse.

"We should think about setting up camp," announced Mouse.
"Let's look at the map and find a good spot."

Moose was happy to follow Mouse.

Mouse was the smart one, after all.

Mouse led Moose through the woods.

By now it was very dark.

"It's a good thing that you reminded me to bring the flashlight," said Moose.

They walked for a long time—
beside the lake, through the woods,
over a bridge, and along a path.

"This looks like a good spot," said Mouse.

Moose nodded in agreement.

Mouse was good at finding places.

Moose unpacked their things.

Mouse told Moose how to put up
the tent.

It was hard work, but Mouse was
good at giving instructions.

"I'm glad you know how to do it!"
said Moose.

Before long Moose and Mouse were
in their sleeping bags.

Mouse took the flashlight and crept out of
the tent.

Mouse seemed to know exactly where he was. And this wasn't surprising—he was in his own backyard!

Mouse let himself in.

He climbed into his own cozy bed.

That night Mouse slept as soundly as ever.

And Moose slept like a log in his

sleeping bag.

In the morning Mouse woke up to the
smell of cooking.

"*That's funny,*" he thought.

Mouse was surprised to find Moose
making breakfast.

"M...m...morning, Moose," said Mouse.

"Morning, Mouse," said Moose.

"It's amazing how we ended up in your

backyard!"

"Y. . . y . . . yes," murmured Mouse.

"In fact," said Moose, "I almost think you did it on purpose!"

And they both chuckled as Moose served breakfast.

The End

About the author and illustrator

Colin West has created over 50 children's books since leaving the Royal College of Art in London, England, in 1975. He enjoys both writing stories and drawing pictures and has published poetry books, storybooks, and picture books. Colin has his own web site, www.colinwest.com. Colin likes the differences between the two friends, Moose and Mouse, but admits, "I'm definitely more like Mouse—I like making up poems, listening to music, and leaving the really hard work to someone else!"

Strategies for Independent Readers

Predict
Think about the cover, illustrations, and the title
of the book. What do you think this book will be about?
While you are reading think about what may
happen next and why.

Monitor
As you read ask yourself if what you're
reading makes sense. If it doesn't, reread, look
at the illustrations, or read ahead.

Question
Ask yourself questions about important ideas
in the story such as what the characters might
do or what you might learn.

Phonics
If there is a word that you do not know, look carefully
at the letters, sounds, and word parts that you do know.
Blend the sounds to read the word. Ask yourself if this is
a word you know. Does it make sense in the sentence?

Summarize
Think about the characters, the setting where the
story takes place, and the problem the characters faced
in the story. Tell the important ideas in the beginning,
middle, and end of the story.

Evaluate
Ask yourself questions like: Did you like the story?
Why or why not? How did the author make the story
come alive? How did the author make the story fun to
read? How well did you understand the story? Maybe
you can understand it better if you read it again!